The Coral Kingdom

To Bea Kenning and Belle 'the best horse in the world'–
I'm sorry there are no horses or ponies in this story but
I hope a very cute seahorse will do instead! – LC

To everyone who helps keep the oceans clean – MO

STRIPES PUBLISHING LIMITED
An imprint of the Little Tiger Group
1 Coda Studios, 189 Munster Road,
London SW6 6AW

A paperback original
First published in Great Britain in 2020

ISBN: 978-1-78895-194-4

2 4 6 8 10 9 7 5 3 1

MERMAIDS ROCK

The Coral Kingdom

Linda Chapman

Illustrated by Mirelle Ortega

Stripes

Contents

Chapter One
The Deep-Water Reef

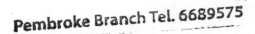

"Watch out, Sami!" Marina exclaimed as a black gulper eel came swimming out of a gloomy cave with its massive mouth wide open. Sami, her pet seahorse, zoomed out of the way just in time. With a flick of her silvery green tail, Marina flattened herself against a coral tree and watched the eel swim past. Its gaping mouth looked almost big enough to swallow her up as well, but luckily it didn't seem interested in eating a mermaid for breakfast!

1

Sami whizzed up to her shoulder, curling his golden yellow tail and hiding behind a strand of her thick brown hair. They watched the eel flick its whip-like body and disappear into the thicket of coral trees, snapping up an unlucky spider crab as it went.

Marina tickled Sami's chest. "That was close!" Sami butted his little head against her finger, his dark eyes shining. She kissed him, making his tiny horns wriggle in delight. He'd been her pet – and best friend – for a year now and she couldn't bear the thought of anything bad happening to him.

"We need to be very careful down here in the deep-water reef," she warned. "There are all sorts of strange creatures around and some of them will be dangerous. It's not like the shallow-water reefs we're used to."

Marina shifted the seaweed bag on her shoulder. She'd travelled around the oceans with her merman dad for all of her eleven years. He was a marine scientist who specialized in studying rare species and they had been to some amazing places together – Pacific atolls, kelp forests in the Norwegian fjords, tropical coastlines... However, this was the first deep-water reef she had visited. The water was much colder this far below the surface of the sea. It was a gloomy world of mountains and crevasses and caves, and wherever she looked there were mounds of grey, dead coral topped with a blanket of living purple, yellow, blue and red coral bushes and feathery pale anemones.

Her dad had told her that some of the tunnels in the reef led to the Midnight Zone and then went even further down to the Abyss – the deepest trenches of the ocean. It was said that some incredibly ancient sea creatures lived in the Abyss but no one had ever been there – and returned. Marina shivered. She loved exploring but even she didn't want to go that far down! The eerie, twilight world of the deep-water reef was exciting enough.

"I wonder where Dad is," she said to Sami as they weaved in and out of the orange coral trees that stretched their branches up towards the surface. A shoal of large fish swam by, their fins flicking against Marina's tail as they passed, and a couple of spiny lobsters picked their way across the sandy bottom.

Marina kept her eyes open for the pot of green mermaid fire that her dad always carried with him to help him see by. "I hope we find him soon," she said to Sami. "I don't want to be late for my first day at school." Excitement curled in her tummy. School! It had been a couple of years since she and her dad had stayed long enough in one place for her to go to school and she couldn't wait. She was really looking forward to making friends and settling down.

Marina and her dad had arrived at Mermaids Rock a few days ago, moving into a large coral cave on the shallow reef where the turquoise water was warm and light and lots of friendly sea creatures lived alongside the merpeople – dolphins, turtles, octopuses and manatees as well as thousands of darting rainbow-coloured fish. It was a beautiful place. Her dad had said they were going to stay for a while so that he could do some research in the deep-water reef that was near to Mermaids Rock, and that suited Marina just fine!

Sami's nostrils widened and he suddenly zoomed ahead of her. He raced off and then came charging back. He bobbed up and down in front of her nose and spun in a circle. Marina grinned at his excitement. "Have you found Dad?"

Sami nodded and led the way. As they rounded the corner, Marina saw a stone

pot of glowing green mermaid fire next to a
cave entrance. Her dad was crouching beside
it, gently scraping a sample of sea moss into
a collecting jar. His tail was a similar silvery
green to Marina's and they both had the same
thick brown hair.

"Dad!" Marina called. Her dad jumped and looked round. "You forgot this," she said, opening her bag and pulling out the packed lunch she had made him the night before. Her dad was great but he did sometimes get so caught up in his research that he forgot about normal things like eating.

"Oh, did I?" Tarak Silverfin looked surprised. He peered inside the bag that was lying next to him. "Barnacles! I did."

Marina sighed. Sometimes she thought her dad would forget his own tail if it wasn't part of him! She handed him the sandwiches. She had brought him some seaweed biscuits as well.

"Thanks, sweetie," he said. "Are you going to stay and help me?"

Marina gave him a hug. "No, it's my first day at school, remember?"

"School?" her dad echoed, looking surprised. "Oh yes. I'd forgotten that was starting today. Should I be coming with you?"

he asked slightly uncertainly.

"No, don't worry. It's fine." Marina was used to doing things on her own that other mergirls and merboys usually did with their parents. In fact, she was so used to looking after her dad that sometimes she felt like she was the parent and he was the child!

"I've got everything sorted. Sami's going to come to the entrance with me and then he'll swim home and wait there." Sami nudged her hand hopefully. "No, you can't come into school with me. I've already told you that," she said. "I know you want to but I'm not allowed to take a pet."

Sami's horns drooped.

"You can come and meet me afterwards though," Marina added.

Sami's horns pricked up again and he turned a happy somersault.

"Right, well, be good, study hard," her dad said vaguely. "All those things."

"I will." Marina kissed him on the cheek.

"I hope your research goes well. You can tell me about it this evening. Watch out for gulper eels though – Sami and I almost got eaten by one just now."

Her dad looked excited. "A gulper eel? Are you sure? They usually live in deeper water than this."

Marina nodded. "I'm sure that's what it was. It had the biggest mouth I've ever seen!"

"Then that probably means that somewhere around here there's a tunnel leading to the Midnight Zone," said her dad. He rubbed his hands together. "This is going to be the perfect place for my research." A frown crossed his face. "You will be careful when you're down here though, won't you? I don't want you to get hurt."

"Don't worry about me. I'll be fine," Marina said. "See you later, Dad!" Swishing her tail, she headed back up towards the surface. She felt like turning a happy somersault just like Sami had. School… New friends… She could hardly wait!

Chapter Two
New Friends

With a flick of her tail, Marina headed in the direction of Mermaids Rock. The merpeople lived on a shallow-water coral reef in a remote part of the ocean, far away from any humans. The entrance to their reef was marked by a huge, submerged rock shaped just like a mermaid's tail. A magic whirlpool swirled round at its base. The merpeople could use it to get to any ocean in the world. All they had to do was touch the rock and say where they wanted to go and then the water would swirl faster.

When they dived into the whirlpool, they were transported away. The merpeople used it to travel to different oceans to help birds and sea creatures that were in danger and to repair damage caused by tidal waves or earthquakes. There was always something to do in the ocean!

Two guards swam on either side of the rock, keeping watch for any dangers approaching the reef. One was a merman with brown hair and a beard; the other was a mermaid with dark hair that fell just below her shoulders.

"What are you doing out so early on your own?" the merman asked Marina as she swam over.

"I've been out to see my dad. He's doing research on the deep-water reef. He's a scientist – Tarak Silverfin," Marina explained.

"Oh yes," said the mermaid, giving Marina a warm smile. "You've just moved here, haven't you?"

Marina nodded. "A few days ago."

"Look out for my son, Kai, at school. He's about the same age as you. I'm Indra, by the way."

Marina smiled at her. "Hi, Indra. Nice to meet you."

The merman was looking concerned. "I'm not sure it's wise for a young mergirl to be swimming out in the ocean on her own. There have been sightings of sharks near here during the last day or two."

"You don't need to worry about me," Marina reassured him. "I'll be fine."

She had learned on her travels that most sharks tended to ignore merpeople and leave them alone. There were *some* vicious ones that liked to attack for no reason but her dad had taught her how to box with her fists and tail in case she ever got cornered. Sharks hated being hit on the snout, as Marina had discovered when she found herself trapped in a cave one day with a nasty grey reef shark in the Indian Ocean!

Marina quickly said goodbye. The last thing she wanted was to be told she couldn't go out to the deep-water reef. She was planning on doing some serious exploring there whenever she got the chance.

As she swam through the warm turquoise waters, she saw mermen and mermaids emerging from their cave homes, chatting and laughing as they shepherded mergirls and merboys to school. Turtles paddled past her, along with shoals of small bright fish, hermit crabs scuttled along the ground while tiny, shrimp-like krill darted among the seaweed, trying to avoid being eaten. The reef stretched for miles, a colourful world of branching corals and tube-like sponges.

A school of red-and-purple firefish enveloped Marina. She raced with them for a few seconds before they swirled on across the reef. Laughing with delight, she spun round and headed towards the school – a large turreted building made out of bluey green coral.

"Watch out!" a voice yelled.

Marina swerved out of the way just in time as a dark-haired boy came hurtling past, holding on to the back of a large hawksbill sea turtle.

"Sorry!" he gasped. "Whoa, Tommy!"

The turtle stopped abruptly and the boy catapulted off. "Oh, flippers!" he cried as he shot through the water.

He slowed to a stop and, with a flick of his tail, he righted himself and swam up to Marina. "Hi! You're new here, aren't you?" he said, his face open and friendly.

Marina nodded. "How did you know?"

He gave her a wide grin. "I know everyone! I'm Kai and this is my turtle, Tommy."

"I just met your mum by the rock! I'm Marina and this is Sami," Marina said. Sami bobbed over to Tommy and the two sea creatures sniffed noses before Sami did a delighted jig and zoomed around Tommy's head. "You're so lucky having a pet you can ride."

Kai put his arm round Tommy. "He's not the most obedient but he's absolutely *krill-iant*!"

Tommy nuzzled his hand and then paddled over to Marina. He gave her an enquiring look

17

with his small dark eyes and pawed her arm with one of his stubby front legs. He tilted his head to one side.

"He wants you to scratch under his chin," said Kai.

Marina did so and the turtle started to shake all over. "What's he doing?" she said, her eyes widening in surprise.

"Laughing!" Kai beamed. "Enough, Tommy," he said, tapping the turtle on the shell. "We'd better get to school. I'll show you the way. So, what were you doing out by the rock?"

They chatted as they swam on. Kai was really easy to talk to and seemed impressed when he heard how much she had travelled. Marina hoped everyone was going to be as nice.

When they reached the entrance, they said goodbye to their pets.

Marina kissed Sami. "I'll see you later." The seahorse nuzzled her cheek and whizzed off with Tommy. Kai and Marina swam through the arched gates. There was an area in front of the building where merboys and mergirls of different ages were playing.

"Those are some of my friends!" said Kai, pointing. "Why don't you come and say hello?"

Marina followed him to where three mergirls were swimming. One had a long tail, pale skin, freckles and dark red, wavy hair that looked as if it hadn't been brushed that morning. She was swimming in circles while the other two were examining something inside a box.

"It's another brilliant invention, Naya," said the smaller, younger mermaid. She had dark red hair like the mermaid swimming in circles but hers was long and straight. "You're so clever."

Naya, a mermaid with dark hair in braids, looked really pleased. "Thanks, Luna. The razor-clam shell is ideal for a ramp and I've made it retractable so that's it's easy for us to carry—"

"Hey, you lot! Say hello to our new classmate!" Kai interrupted. "This is Marina. I bumped into her on the way to school." He grinned. "I mean literally bumped into her – I was being pulled along by Tommy!"

"Kai, you and Tommy are going to injure someone soon," said the mermaid who had been swimming in circles. She grinned at Marina. "Hi, I'm Coralie and this is Luna, my cousin." She pointed to the younger mermaid. "She's usually got a book in her hand and a

load of sea creatures following her around."
Luna gave Marina a shy smile. "And that's
Naya," Coralie continued, pointing to the
other mermaid. "She loves anything to do with
science and is always inventing things."

"Coralie's the one who never stays still for
long, talks a lot and tells really bad jokes!"
Naya put in with a grin.

"My jokes aren't that bad! I know, how
about this one… Why are fish so smart?"
Coralie asked Marina.

"I don't know," said Marina.

Coralie grinned. "Because they live in
schools!"

"I did warn you," Naya sighed.

Marina giggled.

"Kai!" a merboy shouted. "Have you done
that homework project on manatees yet?"

"That's Rafi," said Kai. "I'd better go and
talk to him. See you later!" He swam off.

Marina turned to Naya. "So, what have

you been making?" she asked. "My dad's a scientist. He doesn't invent things but he does lots of research, mainly about sea creatures."

"What's his name?" Naya asked.

"Tarak Silverfin," said Marina.

Naya gasped. "Tarak Silverfin! I've read some of the books he's written. He knows so much about rare species. Oh wow, you're so lucky!"

"You'll have to come and meet him," said Marina.

Naya's brown eyes grew as wide as saucers. "That would be *fin-tastic*!"

"So, what's your invention?" Marina asked curiously.

"It's a special box that we can use to protect sea dragons while they're hatching their young,' said Naya. "Baby sea dragons are so small they quite often get gobbled up by fish soon after they're born so we've been trying to find ways to protect them." She smiled at the other two mergirls. "Luna, Coralie, Kai and I love all sea creatures. In fact, we've just started a club. It's called the Save the Sea Creatures Club."

"You can join if you want," Luna said eagerly. "We're going to go to the reef and look for sea dragons after school."

"That sounds cool!" said Marina.

There was a splutter of laughter behind her. "Cool? I think the words you're looking for are *completely sad*!"

Marina turned and saw a mergirl with waist-length blond hair swimming behind her. She had two other mergirls with her. Her blue eyes gleamed in a way that reminded Marina of the grey reef shark she had fought off.

"You're new, aren't you?" the mermaid said, looking Marina up and down. "I'm Glenda Seaglass and if you want to be popular around here I'd advise you to avoid these losers."

Marina saw Luna and Naya duck their heads and Coralie fold her arms defensively.

"I mean, look at them," Glenda went on as her friends sniggered. "One who looks like she's been dragged through a shipwreck backwards, one who's a science nerd, and a bookworm who usually has some weird creature or other following her around."

"Go away, Glenda," said Coralie angrily. "Don't be mean!"

Glenda ignored her. "Your dad's that famous scientist, isn't he?" she said to Marina. "Well, I suppose you can hang out with me and my friends if you want." She said it as if she was granting Marina a huge favour. "Of course, you won't be able to –" she mimicked Luna's voice – "*join their club*." She glanced at her friends and they giggled. "What a pity!" She motioned with her head. "Come on, come with us."

Marina had no intention of being friends with a girl like Glenda. In fact, she was fighting the urge to bop her on the nose just like she had done with the reef shark!

"No, thanks," she said firmly. "I think the Save the Sea Creatures club sounds like fun. Far more fun than hanging around with someone who thinks it's OK to make horrible comments."

Glenda gaped like a fish. "How … how dare you?"

"Oh, I dare," said Marina coolly. She had no time for bullies.

"You'll be sorry for this, new girl!" Glenda spat. With a flick of her long hair, she swam off. Her friends hurried after her.

Marina shrugged. "You know, somehow I don't think I will be." She turned and saw Coralie, Luna and Naya staring at her in awe.

"You just told Glenda Seaglass you didn't want to be friends with her," breathed Naya.

"She seemed mean." said Marina, shrugging. "I don't like mean people." She looked at them hopefully. "But can I be friends with you?"

"Oh yes!" they chorused, swishing their tails in delight.

"*Fin-tastic!*" Marina beamed. "So, tell me all about this Save the Sea Creatures Club…"

As the others started to chatter happily about how they wanted to protect and look after endangered sea creatures, Marina glanced across to where Glenda had stopped. The blond mergirl was glaring at her. Marina sighed. It looked like she'd made an enemy already. But she'd also made three friends – four including Kai – and being part of the Save the Sea Creatures Club sounded much more fun than hanging out with Glenda and her sneering gang! Marina's first day was going even better than she had expected. Maybe she and the others could even have adventures together while protecting rare sea creatures. She flicked her tail fin happily. Oh yes, that would be the most fun of all!

Chapter Three
Time to Explore!

"So, what does everyone do here after school?" Marina said to Kai when classes finally ended that day. She'd enjoyed all the lessons – marine mammals, conservation of the coral reef, mer-myths, human studies – but she felt like she'd been sitting still for too long and she was ready to do something adventurous.

"Usually, we take our pets for a swim," said Kai.

Naya nodded. "And, while we're out, we clean up any litter that has drifted on to our reef on the ocean currents. We're a long way from any humans but their plastic often ends up here still and then fish and other creatures get tangled up in it or eat it."

"If we find any ill or injured creatures, we take them to the Marine Sanctuary near school," said Luna. "My mum works there."

"Sometimes we play hide-and-seek or have swimming races while we're exploring," said Coralie eagerly.

"But Coralie always wins those," put in Luna.

"Unless I'm riding Tommy!" said Kai with a grin. "Talking of which…" He pointed ahead to the entrance. "There he is! Hey, Tommy!" He waved and swam over to the school entrance where Tommy was paddling beside a grey manatee with gentle eyes set far apart, a dark green octopus with eight waving arms and a young bottlenose dolphin. Sami was bobbing alongside them.

Marina raced over. "Sami!" The little seahorse swam into her hands. She lifted him up to her face and he nudged her nose before curling his tail round a strand of her hair and floating beside her shoulder. She sighed happily. She'd had a lovely day at school but she really had missed him. She was glad he'd made friends with her friends' pets though!

Glancing around, Marina saw that Luna was cuddling the manatee, Naya was talking excitedly to the octopus, Coralie and the dolphin were chasing each other in circles and Kai was racing after them, clinging to Tommy's shell.

"Are these your pets?" she asked.

"Yes, this is Octavia," Naya said. The octopus winked and waved one of her arms. "Luna's manatee is called Melly," Naya continued. Melly gently nudged Marina with her head. Marina stroked her and the manatee immediately rolled over in the water so Marina could scratch her round tummy.

"You're lovely," Marina told her.

"And this is Dash," said Coralie, swerving to a stop with Dash the dolphin next to her. His mouth opened in a wide grin and he clicked his tongue.

When the greetings were over, Marina looked around. "What should we do now? How about we go out to the deep-water reef? That would be fun!" She waited for them to agree with her but, to her surprise, they hesitated.

"Well, we had planned to look for sea dragons on the reef here," said Naya.

"To see if Naya's invention works," added Coralie.

"Oh yes," said Marina, remembering they had told her that before school began.

"And I'm not allowed to go to the deep reef," added Luna. "Mum says I'm not old enough. But you could all go. I can't stay out long anyway tonight – I've got book club later."

"I know, how about we go and look for sea dragons until Luna has to go home and then go and explore the deep-water reef?" Kai suggested.

Coralie, Naya and Luna nodded. Marina

hesitated for a moment but then joined in. She was so used to being on her own, it was a bit strange to have to do what other people suggested! But she did like having friends – she'd just have to get used to it. "Show me where to go," she said cheerfully.

The others led the way, taking her through the world of brightly coloured coral, passing strange-shaped rocks covered in barnacles and anemones and weaving round enormous red sea fans. They peered into caves and into the hollows in the twisting coral. They didn't find any sea dragons but they did see plenty of other creatures.

"Watch out for the urchins ahead!" Coralie warned as they approached a carpet of pink-and-white sea urchins on the sandy seabed. They swam higher – no one wanted a sea-urchin spike in their tail! But Marina caught sight of a plastic bag caught on the spines of one of the sea urchins. She dived down and plucked it off, stuffing it into her school bag. "I hate plastic!" she said. It did so much damage in the oceans.

"Me too," said Naya. "I wish someone would invent something to get rid of it all."

"Look over there!" said Kai suddenly. There was a commotion on the seabed ahead of them. A baby dolphin had got its head and flippers caught in a piece of blue plastic netting. Its mother was circling above, whistling anxiously.

"We need to rescue it!" said Coralie. "Luna! Can you do anything?"

Marina wondered why Coralie was asking the younger mergirl. "I can try to help it," she offered.

"No, wait. Just watch Luna!" said Naya, taking her arm.

They stopped with their animals while Luna swam close to the dolphin and started to hum. As the baby dolphin heard the humming, it gradually stopped thrashing around. Its dark eyes found Luna's and the panic seemed to leave it. She swam closer, still humming softly. "There we are," she murmured as it watched her trustingly. "It's going to be OK – relax." Humming once more, she stroked the dolphin's back. It lay still and let her untangle the netting from its head and flippers. Its mother had stopped panicking too and watched closely.

"There, you're free," said Luna as she put the netting in her bag. The baby dolphin pushed its head into her arms and the mother dolphin gratefully nuzzled Luna's dark red hair.

Marina was astonished. Although wild sea creatures didn't tend to be scared of merpeople, they usually stayed out of their reach. These two dolphins were acting as if they were as tame as Dash. "How did Luna do that?" she breathed.

Naya shrugged. "Sea creatures love her. That's why they follow her around."

"Look," said Kai, nodding to where a blue-and-red slipper lobster was edging its way across the sand towards the little mergirl who was still sitting on the sand, stroking the dolphin. A seahorse bobbed out from a tangle of seaweed and perched on her shoulder. The lobster climbed on to her lap. Luna petted them.

"I'm afraid I've got to go now," she said. "Try to stay away from plastic things." She placed the lobster gently on the rocks, put the seahorse back among the seaweed and kissed the baby dolphin. Then she swam back to the others.

"That was *fin-credible*!" said Marina as Luna swam up to her.

Luna looked pleased. "Thanks! I want to work at the Marine Sanctuary when I'm older like my mum does."

"You'll be *foam-azing* at it," said Coralie, smiling at her little cousin. She chuckled and nudged her. "Hey, what do you call a lazy lobster?" she said, nodding towards the slipper lobster.

"What?" said Luna.

"A *slob*-ster!" Coralie swished her tail and shot away as they all groaned. "I think we should play hide-and-seek! Bagsie not It though!"

"I'll be It," offered Kai. "Go on, all of you. Hide quickly! I'm a fast counter…"

They had a brilliant time playing hide-and-seek and the pets joined in too. Melly, Tommy and Dash were pretty easy to find but Sami could hide in the smallest of places. Marina soon learned that Octavia liked to cheat by blowing out a cloud of black ink and zooming off as soon as she thought she'd been spotted!

When it was time for Luna to go home, the others called goodbye and headed out to the deep reef. Kai's mum, Indra, was still on guard there with the older merman.

"Should you four youngsters really be going out into the ocean on your own?" the merman said, frowning.

"They'll be fine, Rohan," said Indra. "There haven't been any shark sightings today. Do keep a lookout though," she said to Kai. "If you see anything worrying, head straight back here."

"We will, Mum," he said and, with a wave, he raced off. The others followed him, their long tails flicking.

"My dad will probably still be on the deep reef," said Marina.

"I can't wait to meet him!" said Naya. "I've got so many questions I want to ask."

Reaching the deep reef, they dived down. The deeper they swam, the colder and murkier the water got. Compared to the shallow reef, the deep reef was a world of pale coral with just the occasional bright splash of colour – an electric-blue starfish, a glowing purple-and-green jellyfish and a cluster of cylindrical pink sea squirts. It was much quieter and stiller than the bustling shallow-water reef and there seemed to be far fewer creatures, but Marina knew that was because many of the creatures and fish that lived in the deep reef stayed in caves by day and came out to feed at night. She led the way through a gloomy forest of tall coral trees that towered upwards. The silence seemed eerie.

"My dad was near here this morning," said Marina, spotting the caves.

"I heard that some of those caves have tunnels that lead all the way down to the Midnight Zone and then even deeper into the Abyss," said Kai. He tapped Tommy's shell. "No swimming into one of those, Tommy!"

The turtle shook his head.

"I wonder what we'd find if we went to the Midnight Zone," said Coralie. "Sea serpents, giant squid, sea monsters…"

Dash whistled.

"It's OK," she said, patting him. "We won't go there. I know it's too deep for you."

"It would be really fascinating to explore there though," Naya said longingly.

Marina swam to one of the caves and looked inside. "I wonder if this cave has a tunnel in… Oh, flippers!" she gasped. "What's happened here? Look, everyone!"

The others joined her. It was very dark inside the large cave but they could make out that it was completely smashed up inside. Chunks of coral had been torn off the walls and ceiling and lay scattered on the ground. There was a tunnel at the back of the cave that looked as if something heavy had smashed out of it: the shadowy entrance was jagged and broken. Bluey green, tube-shaped sponges that had once grown just inside the cave had been flattened and crushed, and the coral around the entrance to the cave was cracked and wobbly.

"What did this?" said Kai in astonishment.

"Something very strong," said Marina.

"And dangerous," said Coralie. "What creature would just wreck a cave for the sake of it?"

Dash and Tommy made alarmed clicking noises while Sami hid in Marina's hair and Octavia wrapped her arms round Naya's neck.

"I think we should fetch your mum, Kai," said Naya, looking worried. "The guards need to know. There may be something dangerous on the reef."

"I'll go and get them with Dash," said Coralie. "We can swim the fastest."

"OK, we'll wait here," Marina agreed.

Coralie and Dash raced away.

"Marina," Kai said suddenly. "You said your dad was down here. Do you think he's OK?"

A chill ran over Marina's skin. Her dad! Where was he? "I've got to find him!" she said in alarm.

Chapter Four
Chief of
the Guards

"We'll help you look for your dad," Naya said to Marina. "The animals too."

They split up. Octavia, Tommy and Sami went to search among the coral trees while Marina checked in the caves with Kai and Naya.

"Look at this," Naya said, coming out of the damaged cave. She was holding a flat, diamond-shaped object. It was as big as her hand and a smooth, shimmering, silvery blue on one side. "What do you think it is?" she asked, handing it to Marina.

Marina examined the object. It was as hard as rock and about as thick as two of her fingers. She'd never seen anything like it before. "I've no idea," she said. "Maybe it's a weird type of coral?"

Naya tapped it with her finger. "No, it's far too strong and smooth. Some sort of rock or fossil maybe?"

Marina shrugged. Right now, she was more concerned about finding her dad than figuring out what the strange object was.

Tommy and Sami came racing back. Tommy took hold of Kai's arm with his mouth, tugging gently, and Sami bobbed in front of Marina's face before whizzing forwards and waggling his horns.

"I think they want to show us something," said Kai.

Marina shoved the strange object in her bag and they quickly followed Sami and Tommy until they came to a place where coral trees had been knocked over and coral bushes smashed to pieces.

"Whatever damaged the cave must have done this as well!" said Marina.

Octavia came zooming back towards them, her arms flying out behind her. She shook her head at Naya.

"I think she's saying that she followed the trail of broken coral but didn't find anything," said Naya.

Octavia nodded hard.

"Look!" said Naya, swooping down and picking up something flat and silvery by one of the fallen trees. "It's another of those strange things. What are they?"

Just then Dash came swimming down from above, closely followed by Coralie and five guards all armed with tridents including the Chief Guard, a merman called Razeem, and Kai's mum, Indra. Chief Razeem had a dark beard, short brown hair and sharp blue eyes. "Where is this damaged cave?" he demanded.

"Over there, Chief Razeem," said Kai,
pointing back to the caves.

"There's all this damage too," said Marina,
sweeping her arm round at the fallen trees.

Indra came over to the gang as Naya took
Chief Razeem and the other guards to the
cave. "Are you OK?" she asked anxiously.

They nodded.

"I'm worried about my dad though," said

Marina. "He was here this morning and now I can't find him."

"It's OK," said Indra. "Your father went home at lunchtime. He stopped to chat with me for a few minutes. He said he'd found some interesting samples and was taking them to study."

Marina felt relief rush through her. "Oh phew!" she gasped. "I'm glad he's safe."

Chief Razeem came swimming back with the guards and Naya.

"Chief Razeem, what do you think caused this damage?" asked a guard.

"Sharks," Razeem declared.

Marina frowned. "Sharks?"

"Yes," sniffed Razeem. "Two whale sharks were spotted out in the ocean near here yesterday. I bet my tail fin that they're to blame. Whale sharks are big enough to cause this kind of damage and they are vicious, violent creatures."

"They aren't!" protested Marina. "Grey reef sharks and tiger sharks can be aggressive but whale sharks are gentle. They wouldn't do something like this."

Razeem glared down his nose at her as if she was no bigger than a shrimp-like krill. "What could you possibly know about sharks, girl?"

"Well, I've travelled a lot with my dad," said Marina, "and we've met different sorts of sharks. Most of them are quite gentle and even the aggressive ones wouldn't damage a cave for no reason. They're really intelligent creatures and—"

Razeem interrupted her. "Enough! You are a child and you have no idea what you're talking about."

Marina bristled at his words. She saw Indra give her a sympathetic look.

"Sharks are violent and vicious," Razeem went on. "That's all there is to it. Guards, ready your tridents and find those whale sharks. Chase them away from here by whatever means necessary. Meanwhile, you merchildren must return to the safety of the home reef. Take your animals with you."

Coralie, Naya and Kai obediently started to swim away. Marina didn't move though. "Don't chase the whale sharks, Chief Razeem. I'm sure they didn't do this. They prefer being in open water and not down on reefs, and look…" She held up the large silvery objects they had discovered. "We found these. Maybe they're clues—"

"Silence!" Razeem roared. "Get out of here!"

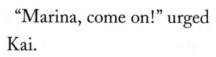

"Marina, come on!" urged Kai.

Marina hesitated. She wasn't used to being ignored, particularly when she knew she had found something important. "But—"

"Marina," interrupted Indra, swimming over to her. "You've been a great help but I think you should go with the others." She glanced at Chief Razeem's furious face. "Go on."

Kai tugged Marina's arm insistently. Marina sighed but let herself be pulled away. She could see the chief wasn't going to listen to her.

"I can't believe you just argued with Chief Razeem," said Naya in awe as they swam off.

"It's not a good idea," said Kai. "He's pretty powerful and Mum says he's got a hot temper."

"But he's wrong!" Marina exclaimed. "Oh, I hope the guards aren't mean to the whale sharks."

"Don't worry. They'll just chase them away," said Kai. "My mum would never hurt a gentle sea creature."

Marina frowned. She didn't even like to think of the whale sharks being frightened.

"Marina, if it wasn't sharks, then what do you think it was?" asked Coralie.

"I don't know," Marina admitted. "I can't think of any sea creatures that go around destroying things for no reason."

"Do you think it could have been a sea serpent?" said Kai. He grabbed Tommy's shell and let himself be pulled along. "Or a giant squid!"

"We could ask your dad if he has any ideas," Naya suggested to Marina.

"Ooh yes," said Marina. It was a mystery and she was determined to solve it. "Let's go and ask him now!"

The cave that Marina and her dad lived in had a large living space with three smaller caves leading off it – two bedrooms and a study. In the centre of the living space was a huge pot of flickering green mermaid fire. The jutting-out coral on the walls of the cave formed natural shelves. They were filled with shell plates and stone beakers as well as objects that Tarak and Marina had collected on their travels – unusual fossils, pearls and pieces of polished sea glass. There were some massive, comfy, orange-and-purple sea sponges scattered over the floor to sit on and a red-and-orange rug woven from seaweed. Marina had also threaded small cowrie shells on to ribbon seaweed and had used them to decorate the walls to make the cave look pretty. She'd made curtains in the same way and hung them over the entrances to the two bedrooms.

Marina swam to the study. "Dad!" she

called. Her father looked round from where he was peering at a sea urchin on his coral desk.

"Hello, sweetie. Has school finished?"

"School finished ages ago," Marina told him. She gave him a hug, remembering how worried she had been down in the deep-water reef. "I'm glad you're safe."

Her dad looked surprised. "Why wouldn't I be?"

Marina told him what had happened.

"Clattering clams, I didn't see a thing!" Tarak Silverfin said. "But the reef covers a huge area and goes far down into the ocean so maybe it's not surprising. It really is a fascinating place, Marina. So many species live there – species we know so little about..."

"Dad, wait," Marina said. When her dad started enthusing about reefs, it was very hard to stop him. "I made some friends at school today. They're here now. Why don't you come and meet them?" She pulled him by the hand into the living space where the others were waiting.

"This is Kai, Coralie and Naya," Marina said, introducing them. "Everyone, this is my dad, Tarak Silverfin."

"Oh my goodness, hello!" gasped Naya. "I think you're amazing, Mr Silverfin! I've read lots of your articles on sea creatures and coral reefs and how we need to protect them."

"Really?" said Tarak, looking pleased.

"Yes," said Naya, nodding hard. "I'd love to be a scientist or an inventor or an engineer when I'm older. Marina told us you're researching the deep-water reef."

"Yes, it's an incredibly diverse ecosystem," said Tarak, his eyes gleaming. "So many species live, breed and bring up their young there. Some of them are incredibly rare. I believe the deep reef may be just the place to find coelacanths."

"*Seel-a-canths?*" echoed Coralie, pronouncing the word in the way Marina's dad just had. "What are they?"

"They're big, armoured fish that are sometimes called living fossils as they're one of the oldest species in the world," Naya answered eagerly. "They can grow up to two metres long, with very hard, bony scales just like fish in prehistoric times had. People used to think coelacanths had been extinct for millions of years but then some live ones were found, weren't they?" she said to Tarak.

He nodded. "Yes, but only a few of them and no one has really managed to study them as a species yet so we still know almost nothing about their habits. I think an untouched deep-water reef like the one close to here might be just the place to find them."

"It would be *foam-tastic* to really be able to study them! They're dark blue, aren't they? With pale spots?" Naya said.

"They are! I have a very good picture of one in my study. Would you like to see it?" Tarak asked.

"Oh, yes please," breathed Naya.

Tarak swam into his study with Naya following him.

Marina shook her head. "Well, I guess we won't be seeing them for a while."

Coralie grinned. "Naya looked like she was about to pop with delight! We're never going to hear the end of this."

"What should we do while we're waiting?" said Kai.

Marina plonked herself down on one of the squishy sponges. "We must try to solve the mystery of the damaged cave!" she exclaimed.

Chapter Five
A Mystery to Solve

"What clues have we got?" Marina began. "There was a lot of damage, which means whatever the creature is it's something big and strong."

"Strong enough to knock over a coral tree," agreed Kai.

Dash was lying next to Coralie and she had her arm over his body. He opened his mouth and whistled. "Yes, that's right, Dash. It would need sharp teeth to have been able to tear the coral out of the cave walls," she said.

"And there were those two silvery things," she continued, getting them out of her bag. "Look, what are they?"

"They're made up of layers," said Kai, taking one from her and looking closely at the edge. "And the shiny side feels a bit like the surface of a tooth."

"If it's a tooth, it's the strangest tooth I've ever seen," said Coralie, examining the object and looking at it from every angle. "What creature has flat, diamond-shaped, silver teeth?"

"It might not even be anything to do with the creature," said Kai.

"We should count it as a clue though," said Marina. "Maybe Dad will have some ideas about what's going on down on the reef. Dad!" she called. "We need your help!"

Tarak swam through with Naya and Marina explained what they were doing. "What could have done so much damage?"

"Crown of thorns starfish can destroy sections of a reef in days," said Tarak. "They feed on the coral."

"But they wouldn't be able to knock down coral trees," said Kai.

"No," said Tarak. "And generally they prefer shallow, warmer water."

"We found this," Coralie said, holding up the strange object. "But we don't know what it is."

"There were two of them," said Naya.

"How fascinating," said Tarak, studying the object. "It's shaped like a type of fish scale but it's much too big and heavy to be one. Its surface seems to be made of a sort of enamel. I've no idea what it is."

Marina sighed. "We're not getting much closer to working out what really happened."

"I'll keep my eyes open when I'm at the reef tomorrow," said her dad.

"Do you think a sea monster might have damaged the cave?" Kai said. "My cousins once told me about a sea monster that came up through the tunnels and swam to our reef. It liked to eat mergirls and merboys!"

Tarak smiled. "The ocean hides many creatures in its depths and I'm sure some of them could be classed as sea monsters. However, I very much doubt they would come to this reef and eat merpeople. I think they'd stay deep in the ocean, far away from the shallow reefs." He rubbed his chin. "This is a real puzzle."

"Well, we're going to solve it!" Marina declared.

"Did you hear about the attack on the deepwater reef yesterday?" Glenda's shrill voice was triumphant as she talked to a group of mergirls and merboys outside school the following day when Marina arrived with Kai. "Sharks were to blame. My dad realized straight away.

He found the sharks and chased them away. But then, of course, he is Chief of the Guards." She looked even more smug than usual.

"Chief Razeem is Glenda's father?" Marina whispered to Kai.

He nodded. "Yep, and no one's allowed to forget it."

"Did your dad really chase two sharks away on his own?" said one of Glenda's friends, looking impressed.

Glenda nodded.

"She's lying," muttered Kai to Marina. "My mum was there and the other guards."

"Your dad's so brave," another mermaid said to Glenda.

Glenda smirked. "He is and he says I'm just like him."

"I'd like to see Glenda chase a shark," hissed Kai. "I bet if she saw one, she'd swim away as fast as a jet-propelled squid!"

Just then Luna and Coralie arrived.

"Kai! Marina!" cried the younger mergirl, swimming up to them. "Coralie told me that when you went to the deep-water reef yesterday you found the damaged cave that everyone's talking about. Weren't you scared? Coralie says it might have been destroyed by a sea monster!" Her eyes were wide.

The mergirls and merboys listening to Glenda turned round.

"You lot were at the caves?" said one.

"You actually saw the damage?" said another, swimming over. "What was it like?"

"Horrible," said Kai dramatically. "There

were chunks of coral everywhere." He waved his hands in the air, his eyes lighting up as he began to tell the story. "All these trees had been knocked over. It was like a massive sea monster or sea serpent had swum through the reef. I don't know what did it but at one point I thought I saw a huge dark shadow disappearing into the distance."

Everyone surrounded him.

"Really?"

"What was it like?"

"Did it have big teeth?"

Glenda looked very cross that she had lost her audience. "It was just a couple of whale sharks. My dad found them both and chased them away!" she said loudly.

But no one was listening to her any more apart from her two best friends, and even they were edging closer to hear Kai's story.

"Were there teeth marks in the coral? My mum says there were," said one merboy.

"Really, really big ones," said Kai, getting carried away. "Gigantic fang marks! You should have seen them!"

"I bet it *was* a sea monster!" breathed one of the other mermaids. "One that eats merpeople!"

Glenda frowned. "Why are none of you listening to me? It was a whale shark. And it's very lucky my dad got rid of it or we might all be in danger!"

"No, we wouldn't," said Marina. "Whale sharks don't hurt merpeople. They're actually very gentle."

"What do you know about sharks?" scoffed Glenda. "My dad says sharks are vicious and he knows a lot more than you!" Turning, she swam off with her two friends. As she passed Luna, she spitefully flicked Luna's tail from under her, making the younger mergirl somersault over in the water. Marina caught up with Glenda and swerved in front of her, making the other mergirl stop abruptly.

"I saw that!" she said through gritted teeth.

"What?" Glenda said, looking innocent.

"I saw you tip Luna over," said Marina, holding out her hand and helping Luna right herself.

"You didn't see me do anything, did you?" Glenda said to her friends.

"Definitely not," they chorused smugly.

"You're as blind as a hagfish, Marina." Glenda smirked. "You should get your eyes tested."

"She's as ugly as one too!" giggled one

of Glenda's friends.

Marina ignored her and swam closer to Glenda. "I know what you did. Don't you dare hurt Luna again!"

"Ooh, I'm so scared," said Glenda but she fidgeted uncomfortably under Marina's glare. "Come on," she said to the others, putting her nose in the air. "It stinks around here."

They swam away.

"Thank you," Luna said, taking Marina's hand.

Marina squeezed it. "She's such a bully. Try not to let her get to you."

They returned to Kai who was now busy telling everyone how they'd followed the shadowy creature before losing it in the trees. Marina listened, half wishing that everything Kai was making up had really happened. It sounded very exciting!

"So, have you or your dad had any more ideas about what the creature might be?" asked Naya, swimming up beside her with Coralie.

"No," said Marina.

"We could always go back after school today," said Coralie, her eyes gleaming, "and see if we can find any more clues."

"No, don't!" said Luna in alarm. "It sounds much too scary."

Marina gave her a reassuring smile. "Don't worry, we'll be fine. I've travelled to lots of places with my dad and know how to be careful." She turned to the others. "So, do you really want to go back to the deep reef after school and try to solve the mystery?"

"Definitely!" Coralie and Naya exclaimed.

Chapter Six
Danger on the Reef

After school, Marina, Kai, Naya and Coralie headed to the deep reef. Kai's mum was guarding Mermaids Rock again but she was happy to let them past. "The whale sharks have gone now," she said. "I'm sure you'll be OK."

"Thanks, Mum," said Kai.

Marina hesitated but decided it wasn't the time to lecture Kai's mum about whale sharks.

They swam on until they reached the reef. "Let's go to the caves again," said Marina as they reached the gloomy coral forest. The deep reef seemed particularly eerie and dark that day. Although she knew that Kai had made up his story about seeing a sea monster, she found it all too easy to imagine that there might be a large, mermaid-eating monster lurking somewhere in the shadows. A shiver ran down her spine. *You can solve this*, she told herself firmly.

"Be careful, Octavia!" gasped Naya, grabbing the octopus as she almost swam into the long, poisonous spines of a red

scorpionfish resting on a rock.

"There are so many dangerous creatures here," said Coralie as a moray eel came swimming out of the murky water towards them, its mouth open, showing its razor-sharp teeth, making them all swerve to one side.

"Look!" Kai said, pointing through the gloom. "What's that?"

A creature, about the size of a dolphin, was drifting silently in the dark water through the trees behind them.

"It's a fish, I think," said Marina, peering at it. "A really big one with spots."

"It's got more fins than most fish usually have," said Kai. "Look, there are four under its belly and then another four higher up."

"It's swimming backwards!" Coralie pointed out. "That's weird. I've never seen a fish do that before."

Naya gasped. "Marina, I think it's a coelacanth! The type of fish your dad is looking for! They're one of the few fish that can swim backwards and they have four fins on their tummy."

As they watched, the fish flipped itself over so it was pointing vertically downwards, its mouth pressing into the sandy ground in an 'o' shape, its tail pointing straight up towards the surface.

"It can do headstands too!" said Kai in astonishment.

"That's its way of feeding," said Naya.

"It's probably found some krill in the sand. Oh, your dad's going to be so pleased, Marina!" She hurried towards the fish.

The others swam after her but, as soon as the coelacanth saw them approaching, it shot away round a coral tree. When they reached the tree, they couldn't see any sign of it in the dark water.

"Oh," said Naya, disappointed. "It's gone."

"Maybe it went into one of those caves," said Kai, pointing.

Naya nodded. "Coelacanths like to rest in caves during the day. If we can find where it's hiding, we can tell your dad and he can study it," she said to Marina.

"Let's get looking!" said Marina excitedly.

She started searching the caves. The others followed. "Hey! Look at this!" called Coralie from one of the smaller caves. "There's more damage here!" They joined her and saw that something had knocked chunks of coral from the opening. Inside, the cave was just as wrecked as the one the day before. There was a tunnel at the back and the entrance to it was smashed up too.

"It looks like something came out from that tunnel," said Coralie.

"A sea monster," breathed Kai. "Just like I said! It must have come up through the tunnel and burst out of the cave!"

"No…" started Naya. She swam over. "The rocks have mainly fallen into the tunnel, not into the cave, which means something was trying to get *into* the tunnel…"

"Or trying to stop something from coming out of it," said Marina thoughtfully.

They exchanged worried looks.

Octavia swam up to Naya and tugged at her with an arm. "What is it?" she said.

Octavia pulled her to the cave entrance. Marina followed, eager to see what Naya's pet had found. The octopus propelled herself downwards and pointed at the ground. Marina saw there was a strange circle indent in the sand nearby, about a metre across and half a metre deep.

"What do you think it is?" asked Naya.

"I don't know," Marina replied.

"There's another over here," Kai called, following Tommy. He patted the sand crater. "I've never seen marks like this."

BOOM!

There was a loud thundering noise in the distance.

"What was that?" said Naya uneasily.

Two large spotted stingrays came racing out of the trees. They swooped up over the top of the merchildren's heads. They were closely followed by a shoal of silver fish.

BOOM! CRASH!

"W-what's going on?" stammered Coralie as the coral shook with each loud noise. Sami hid in Marina's hair and Tommy, Dash and Octavia swam in panicked circles.

BOOM! CRASH! BOOM!

The noise grew louder.

"Something's coming this way!" Marina realized as a squid raced past them, shooting out a cloud of black ink behind it. "We've got to get out of here – and fast!"

Tommy dived underneath Kai and started to push him upwards through the water. Octavia wrapped four of her arms round Naya's arm and pulled her after Tommy. Dash whistled in panic to Coralie and motioned upwards with his nose.

Marina knew that whatever was coming had to be seriously scary for their pets to be reacting in such a way. There was another crash and the coral around them juddered even more.

"Come on!" she yelled to Coralie, who was hesitating.

The two of them swam after the others as fast as they could. Coralie glanced back at one point and then started to swim even faster. Up and up they went until they broke through the surface of the ocean. They were all panting. The animals swam around, nuzzling against them.

"What – what was that?" said Naya, trying to get her breath back.

"I've no idea," said Marina. She caught Sami in her hands and kissed him. She was very glad they were all safe.

"I looked back as we were swimming away and I'm sure I saw something," said Coralie. "Something massive."

"As big as a whale shark?" asked Naya.

"Even bigger! More the size of a blue whale."

They stared at each other. Blue whales were the biggest creatures in the ocean.

"We should tell my mum," said Kai.

"It must be what's been damaging the caves."

"I knew it wasn't those poor whale sharks!" said Marina.

"Come on," said Naya, looking anxious. "We need to let the guards know about this."

They raced back to Mermaids Rock. When they told Kai's mum what they had seen, she picked up a conch shell from a nearby rock and blew it loudly like a horn.

Soon, all of the guards had gathered and, led by Chief Razeem, they headed down to the deep-water reef. Before they left, they tied a rope of red seaweed round Mermaids Rock. It meant that there was something dangerous happening and everyone else should stay on the shallow home reef and not travel out into the surrounding ocean.

Marina waited anxiously. She hoped the guards would be OK. What would they find down there? Kai had his arm round Tommy's shell and was staring out towards the deep reef. Coralie was swimming in circles with Dash, and Naya was talking to Octavia, looking worried.

"Whatever's going on?" Marina's dad swam up to them with his collecting bags slung over his shoulder. "Why's that red rope up?"

Marina told him what had happened.

"I'm glad you're OK." Her dad's eyes took on a faraway look. "Hmm, I wonder what's down there."

Marina knew that look. He wanted to go and investigate. "You can't go out on the reef, Dad." She pointed to the red rope. "That means everyone has to stay here."

Naya suddenly remembered something. "Mr Silverfin!" she gasped. "You'll never guess what we saw – just before we heard the noise. It was a coelacanth!"

"A coelacanth?" Tarak echoed. "Are you sure?"

Naya nodded. "It was the right size and

colour and we saw it swim backwards and turn vertical in the water. It had four fins attached to its stomach and hard, armoured scales, just like that drawing of a coelacanth you showed me."

"Can you remember where it was?" Tarak asked eagerly. "Could you take me there?"

Marina frowned. She knew the way her dad's mind was working. "Yes, but you can't go now, Dad. No one's allowed to leave the reef."

Her dad frowned in irritation. "Barnacles! This is such bad timing!"

"The coelacanth will still be there later," Marina told him.

"That's true," her dad said, nodding. "I'll go tonight. Coelacanths are most active at night-time anyway. They hate light and much prefer the dark." He rubbed his hands together. "A coelacanth. Oh my!"

However, when the guards returned, Chief Razeem made an announcement that ruined Tarak's plans. He blew three long notes on the conch horn – a signal that all the merpeople on the reef should gather at Mermaids Rock.

"The guards and I have found evidence suggesting that an extremely large, dangerous predator is currently living in the deep-water reef," he said when everyone was present – mermaids, mermen and merchildren. "At the moment we do not know what kind of creature we're dealing with. We just know is that it's something vicious and violent. While we're investigating, no one is to go to the deep reef or out in the ocean."

Everyone started to whisper and speculate. A large predator... Was it a sea serpent ... a giant squid ... an unknown monster from the deep?

"Not go to the deep-water reef!" Marina's dad exclaimed above the noise. "But that's ridiculous, Razeem. I demand to be allowed to carry on with my research."

"There will be no exceptions!" Chief
Razeem snapped. "No one apart from the
guards may go to the deep-water reef until
we have dealt with this creature."

"Chief Razeem!" Marina put up her hand.
He frowned at her. "Yes?"

"How do you know the creature is dangerous?"

"We've seen the damage it's done."

"But you thought it was whale shark and it wasn't. What if you're wrong about this too?"

"Enough, child!" Razeem snapped. "The reef is out of bounds and that's all there is to it. I have nothing more to say!"

Chapter Seven
Missing!

When the meeting ended, Marina's dad swam away home, looking very cross. Marina joined the others. Luna was with them. "You were actually on the reef when the creature appeared?" she was saying. "What if it had attacked you all?"

"We got out of the way pretty quick," said Coralie.

"Did you see it?" Luna asked.

"No, I just saw a big shadow. But you should have heard the noise it made."

"*Boom! Crash!*" said Kai. "It was awesomely scary!"

"I wish we could go back," said Marina. It had been frightening but she was longing to find out more. "I just want to know what it is."

"Something big and strong, with sharp teeth, that doesn't seem to like tunnels, coral trees or caves much!" said Naya, ticking the things off on her fingers. "Oh, and it may make strange circles in the sand. Anyone got any ideas?"

"None at all," said Coralie.

"We'll just have to wait until the guards find out more," said Kai.

Marina sighed in frustration. "But I don't want to wait."

"I know but I think we have to," said Coralie.

Luna tugged at her arm. "The monster won't come here to our reef, will it? Like the sea monster that went to a reef once and ate up the merpeople!"

Coralie gave her a hug. "That's just a story. We're safe here, Luna. The guards will protect us."

"But what about the creatures on the deep reef? Who will protect them?" Luna said anxiously.

"I know, why don't we do something together?" said Marina quickly, realizing they needed to distract the younger mergirl before she got really upset. "Let's go looking for sea dragons again! That's far more fun than just hanging around here." She took Luna's hand and spun her until she laughed. "What do you say, Luna?"

"OK!" Luna gasped.

They headed for the reef. Luna was soon being followed by an assortment of creatures – a seahorse, a stripy triggerfish and a young loggerhead turtle.

"How does this plastic stuff end up in the sea?" Luna said as she swooped down and grabbed a bottle that an orange-and-white clownfish was about to swim into.

"I really don't know," said Marina. "I suppose the humans just don't realize the damage they're doing."

"My mum says that there's more plastic than ever," said Kai. "It's even turning up in really remote oceans."

"What did one ocean say to the other ocean?" asked Coralie.

"What?" Luna said.

"Nothing. They just waved." Coralie giggled as the others groaned.

"When I'm older, I want to visit all the different oceans," said Luna. "As well as working at the sanctuary of course."

"What about you, Marina? What do you want to do?" Naya asked.

"I'm not sure," said Marina. "Maybe do research like my dad."

"I want to be a guard," said Coralie.

"I don't know what I want to do," said Kai, turning a somersault. "Something fun! Speaking of which…" He tapped Marina on the arm and Tommy on the shell. "Let's play tag. You and Sami are the catchers, Marina!"

"Can't catch me!" cried Coralie, diving away.

"Or me!" squealed Luna.

They raced around, playing tag. They didn't stop until they were out of breath and it was time to go home for tea.

"See you tomorrow at school!" Marina called as they swam back to their caves. She and Kai lived close to each other and, as they reached

Kai's cave, his mum came swimming out.

"There you are," she said to Kai. "I was beginning to wonder where you'd got to."

"Did you find anything at the reef, Mum?" Kai asked eagerly.

"No, just lots of damage. There's obviously something very big and dangerous down there at the moment."

"A sea monster?" Kai asked.

"I don't know. Chief Razeem thinks it's something vicious but I'm really not sure. Anyway, he wants the guards to go back there early in the morning." Indra smiled at Marina. "Hopefully we'll sort this out soon, then your dad can get on with his research."

Marina nodded. "He really won't like having to stay away."

Particularly not now he knows we've seen a coelacanth on the reef, she added to herself.

"Bye!" she said. "See you in the morning, Kai." And, with a flick of her tail, she headed home.

Her dad was working in his study when she got in. Marina made seaweed salad for supper and carried some through to him. Tarak was examining one of the silvery objects Naya had found and comparing it to pictures in a book, his desk lit by a pot of mermaid fire.

"Here you are, Dad, supper," Marina said.

Her dad barely even glanced up. "Ah, thank you," he muttered. "These things you found are fascinating, Marina. They seem to be made up of layers of several different types of bone with a hard enamel coating on top – that's the shiny surface. It's very similar to the make-up of a coelacanth's scales but this can't possibly be a scale from a coelacanth. It's the wrong shape and much too large and heavy. So, what is it and where did it come from?" He rubbed his chin. "I need to find that coelacanth you saw on the reef. Studying it may help to shed

93

light on whatever this is." He turned back to his book, his dinner already forgotten.

Marina left him to it. She ate her own seaweed and then curled up on one of the sea sponges beside the glowing pot of mermaid fire. She read a book about an adventurous mermaid who went exploring the frozen waters of the north, meeting polar bears and seals. Sami perched on her shoulder, stroking her cheek with his horns. Marina snuggled deeper into the sponge and yawned. It had been a very long, tiring day and, before she knew it, she was fast asleep.

Marina woke up and for a moment couldn't think where she was. She blinked and realized she had fallen asleep in front of the fire with Sami nestling against her neck. She stretched, wondering why her dad hadn't woken her up and told her to go to bed. She checked the clock on one of the shelves. Five o'clock in the morning! It was dark outside, still night-time.

Marina rubbed her eyes and tickled Sami to wake him up. "We should go to bed and get some more sleep," she said, yawning. "It's too early to get up yet."

She swam up from the sea sponge and he followed her sleepily towards her bedroom. On the way, she pulled back the curtain of shells that separated her dad's bedroom from the living space. Why hadn't he woken her up? Looking in, she realized the thick seaweed blanket was still pulled up neatly over the sea-sponge pillow. He hadn't been to bed at all by the looks of it. He must still be working. She swam to his study.

"Dad!" she called softly, peering inside. "Dad! You really need to go to bed—" She broke off. Her dad wasn't in his study either. Marina frowned, a sudden cold feeling running through her. *Where was he?* Glancing around, she saw his collecting bags had gone – and his pot of mermaid fire.

"Oh no," she whispered in alarm. Sami put his head on one side questioningly. "Sami, I bet Dad went to the reef to try to find that coelacanth!"

She knew just how her dad's mind worked. He'd told her coelacanths were more active at night and so going there after dark would be his best chance of seeing one.

But why hasn't he come back? What if he's in danger?

Marina swallowed. There was only one

thing for it. "I've got to go after him!" she declared. For a moment, she wondered if she should tell someone her plan – she could go and wake Kai – but no, she decided. He'd only try to stop her. It was better if she sorted this out on her own.

Sami looked at Marina in alarm as she filled her own small pot with some mermaid fire – it was so dark, she would need it to see by. As she headed for the cave entrance, Sami swam in front of her. She tried to get round him but he wouldn't let her, dodging from side to side. "What are you doing?" she demanded.

Sami shook his head.

"Sami, I've got to go," she told him.

The little seahorse waggled his horns sternly.

"Dad could be in trouble," Marina said. "I don't know how long he's been gone but there's something dangerous on that reef." She picked the little golden seahorse up in her hands and gently moved him out of the way. "Please stay here. There'll be all sorts of creatures who come out on the deep reef at night and I don't want you to get hurt." She made her voice as firm as she could. "Stay, Sami. I mean it. Stay!"

The seahorse watched her swim out of the cave. Marina felt relieved that he was doing as he was told but she did miss him swimming beside her. Her tummy swirled with nerves.

I'll be back soon, she told herself firmly as she swam towards Mermaids Rock.

The deep-water reef was even spookier at night. Marina had thought it would be almost pitch-black but, as she swam down towards the caves, she realized that many of the sea creatures that came out on to the reef at night-time glowed and shone. There were tiny firefly

squid bobbing
through the
water, each
about the
length of one of
Marina's fingers,
their bodies flashing
with tiny pinpricks of
blue light. There were also
loads of jellyfish, their dome-like
heads shining with purple, green and blue
light, and fish with fangs and strange waving
antennae that lit up like tiny green lanterns.
Even some of the coral seemed to be glowing.

Marina held the pot of mermaid fire out in
front of her as she swam swiftly down. Where
was her dad? For a moment, she had the
horrible feeling that something was following
her. She stopped and glanced around uneasily,
but all she could see were the drifting, glowing
jellyfish. She must have imagined it.

Keep going, she told herself. *You have to find Dad.*

She swam on until she reached the cave near where they had seen the coelacanth. "Dad!" she called softly. "Dad, are you there?" Her eyes scanned the water, looking for the glow of the mermaid fire he had taken with him.

She started to swim in and out of the caves. Reaching the largest damaged cave, she hesitated. The coral around the entrance looked very wobbly and unsafe. "Dad?" she called, swimming inside. But, as she did so, her tail flicked against the edge of the entrance.

CRACK!

The coral splintered and collapsed. Marina squealed as chunks of it rained down with a thundering, crashing sound.

BANG! SMASH!

Swinging round, she looked at the cave mouth in horror. It was completely blocked. She was trapped!

Swimming over to the huge heap of broken coral, she started desperately trying to move chunks away. As Marina pulled out one bit, some fell from above and hit her on the shoulder. Another piece narrowly missed her head. "Ow!" she gasped.

She retreated into the cave, her heart racing. Whatever was she going to do now?

Chapter Eight
Trapped!

Marina tried to stay calm. Someone would come and rescue her. But who? No one knew she was on the deep reef.

Dad will realize I'm missing when he finally gets home, she thought. *But what if he's in trouble too and can't go home?* Her heart sank. Oh, why hadn't she told someone where she was going? Why had she just raced off on her own? She should have let the others know.

The others! she thought. *They're bound to wonder where I am if I don't turn up at school*

*today. I bet they'll go to my cave after classes have
finished and realize I've vanished.*

She sat down on a rock and wrapped her
arms round herself. The end of school seemed
like a long time away and what about her dad?
He might be in trouble and she was trapped
and couldn't help him. Marina glanced at
the dark tunnel at the back of the cave. It
reminded her of a gaping, hungry mouth but
maybe she should try to see if there was a way
out through it?

She swam over. The tunnel led straight
down and the water inside it felt icy cold. The
mermaid fire showed nothing but dark water.
Marina hesitated. She could try swimming
down it. But what if it led all the way to the
Abyss? And what if she started swimming and
then got stuck? She bit her lip. If no one came
to rescue her, she might have to risk it but not
yet. She turned and almost squealed again as
she saw something move in the shadows of the

cave wall. It was a very large fish – about the same size as Marina herself. It was gradually inching out from a hidden crevice in the wall.

Marina took a trembling breath. For a moment, she had thought it might be the sea monster! As more of the fish came into view, she saw that it had hard blue scales all over its body and eight fins altogether – four of them hanging down from its belly.

It was the coelacanth they had seen the day before! This cave must be its hiding place.

She picked up the mermaid fire from the tunnel, intending to have a closer look, but as soon as the fish saw the light it swam backwards and retreated into the crevice.

Marina put the mermaid fire down, remembering that her dad had said coelacanths preferred the dark. She swam slowly over to the crack in the cave. "It's OK, I'm not going to hurt you," she whispered, wishing she had Luna's gift for making sea creatures trust her.

"You can come out." She hoped it would – having a fish for company was much better than being on her own.

The fish's nose poked out of the crevice. It edged out a little and looked at her with its large eyes. Marina carried on talking gently to it. "I really won't harm you. Merpeople help all sea creatures. Please come out."

The fish didn't understand the words she was saying but it seemed to realize from the tone of her voice that she wasn't something to be afraid of. It swam out and Marina looked at it in awe. It was so big and looked different to other fish. She realized the difference was because of its scales. They were hard, like rock, and very different from the thin, delicate scales that covered her own tail.

She held out her hand, hoping it wouldn't bite, but the fish seemed very gentle. Its lips brushed against her fingers and then it blew out a stream of bubbles that floated behind.

It swam to the centre of the cave and then turned upside down, bumping at the bottom of the cave with its mouth. Each time it bumped the sand, it made a circle.

Circles? Marina frowned as a memory stirred in her head. Circles in the sand… What did that make her think of?

"Marina!"

The coelacanth stiffened and turned the right way up at the sound of voices outside the cave.

"Marina?"

"Are you there?"

"Kai! Naya! Coralie!" Marina gasped, swimming to the blocked entrance. She saw the coelacanth disappearing into its crevice again. "Is that you?"

"Yes!" her friends said.

"And me as well!" she heard Luna pipe up.

"How did you know I was here?" Marina demanded.

"It was Sami. He went to Kai's house and woke him up," said Coralie.

"He kept bumping me with his nose and racing to the door," said Kai. "I guessed something must be wrong so I went round to your cave and realized both you and your dad were missing! I went to get the others and then Sami led us here."

"He must have come after me and seen me getting trapped," Marina realized. "I thought something was following me!"

"What happened?" Coralie asked.

Marina explained. "I'm so glad you're here," she finished. "I thought I was going to have to stay in this cave for ages and ages. I don't know where Dad is. I was looking for him when the cave entrance collapsed."

"We need to get you out of there," said Coralie.

"The question is – how?" said Naya.

"Can't we just pull the rocks away and make a large enough space for Marina to get through?" said Kai. "Look, like this!"

Marina felt the wall of coral shake slightly and guessed Kai was pulling pieces of coral away.

"Be careful!" she warned, remembering what had happened when she had done the same. But she was too late. There was a crunching, crashing sound.

"Ow!" she heard Kai exclaim.

"Are you OK, Kai?" Naya said anxiously.

"Kai just got hit by some coral," Coralie explained through the wall to Marina. "He's all right though."

"Maybe we should go and get the guards," said Luna nervously. "Before the sea monster comes along."

"No, it'll take too long to get them and anyway I've had an idea!" said Naya. "What we need to do is push a support beam or prop into the rubble about halfway up – something strong and flat. It would act like a roof, holding up all the coral above it. We'll then be able to take some of the coral underneath it out and make a hole for Marina to wiggle out of without the rest of the coral falling on top of us."

"What do you mean?" Luna said.

"Everyone look for something strong and flat that we could use as a prop," said Naya, "and then I'll show you."

Marina could hear them searching.

"How about this?" said Coralie.

"An old turtle shell – perfect!" said Naya. "Come on, everyone! We need to slide it into the rubble and then take out some of the coral. Animals, you can help too! Tommy, use your flippers and Octavia, your arms. Dash, you and Melly can carry the coral away. We need to be as quick as we can!"

There was the sound of scratching and scraping as the friends worked together to get the turtle shell into the wall and remove some of the coral beneath it.

A small hole appeared in the wall. "It's working!" exclaimed Marina.

The next moment Sami squeezed through into the cave. He bobbed around her, nudging at her face, giving her gentle seahorse kisses. She cupped him in her hands and kissed his nose. "Thank you for getting everyone to rescue me," she told him. "I should be cross with you for not staying at home, but I'm really not!"

He waggled his horns cheekily.

The others were still working away and the hole grew bigger and bigger.

"That's it! I can get out of here now!" Marina cried.

She glanced around. The coelacanth was still hiding but that was fine. It would be safe there. Picking up her pot of mermaid fire, she swam out through the hole and flung her arms round her friends, hugging them tightly. "Thank you, everyone!" she gasped. Melly and Dash nuzzled her while Tommy and Octavia whizzed about in delighted circles.

"I'm so glad you're OK, Marina," said Luna. "It's really scary here."

"I can't believe you're actually here on the deep reef," Marina said to her. "It's so brave of you. Won't your mum be really cross if she finds out?"

"I don't care. When the others said you might be in trouble, I had to come." Luna stroked Melly with her free hand. "I knew Melly would look after me."

The wide-eyed manatee looked pleased.

"Why did you come here by yourself?" Naya said to Marina. "You know you can always ask us for help. It's safer than coming on your own."

"I know. I realized that when the cave mouth fell in. I'm so lucky you're here now," Marina said gratefully.

Tommy swam towards Kai and gestured upwards with his head and a front flipper.

Kai nodded. "Tommy thinks we should get out of here. The monster could appear any moment."

Dash clicked his tongue in agreement. "Let's go," said Coralie.

"But I can't leave," protested Marina. "I need to find my dad. I don't know where he is and why he's been out so long."

"Why don't we go and tell my mum?" said Kai. "She'll know what to—"

BOOM!

They all jumped.

"W-what was that?" said Naya anxiously.

"Is it the sea monster?" Luna looked like she was about to faint.

BOOM!

The coral shook and more chunks fell off. The next moment there was a loud crash as a tree fell, followed by the loudest roar Marina had ever heard.

"We need to get out of here," she said
in alarm. "Before it's too late!" A shoal of
frightened fish came racing through the water
and swerved past just as a massive shadow fell
over them.

"I think it's already too late!" gasped
Coralie. "Quick, everyone! Hide!"

Chapter Nine
The Sea Monster

They dashed inside the nearest cave with their pets. Sami tangled his tail in Marina's hair as they peeped out from the cave's opening.

"Look!" whispered Luna in terror.

An absolutely gigantic creature was swimming very slowly towards the cave. It was covered in rock-hard, diamond-shaped, silvery blue scales each as big as Marina's hands. Marina noticed that two were missing... The strange objects they had found must have been scales from this creature! It had four enormous

fins hanging under its body. It looked like
a fish but it was far bigger than even the
coelacanth and had a longer neck than a
normal fish. It opened its mouth to roar again,
revealing a row of ferocious-looking teeth.

"There really are such things as sea
monsters after all!" gulped Kai.

Luna grabbed Marina's hand. "Do you
think it will eat us?"

"Look at those teeth!" whispered Naya.

CRASH!

The creature's tail fin hit a coral tree and smashed it to pieces.

"Oh, barnacles!" whispered Coralie, wrapping her arms round Dash. "We're going to be a monster's dinner!"

The creature's yellow eyes glanced from side to side. It looked...

Marina frowned. Not vicious. Not aggressive. It looked worried – confused. She stared at the four fins attached to the creature's belly and at the hard scales that covered its body and felt a memory stir in her mind. The enormous creature suddenly turned vertical, its tail pointing up to the surface, its massive teeth crunching into the sand as it created an enormous, deep crater. Circles in the sand... Of course! Marina gasped.

"It's not a monster, everyone! I think it's just a ginormous coelacanth!"

"Oh, it could be a megacoelacanthus!" Naya breathed. "They're from the same family as the coelacanth. They were in the oceans at the time of the dinosaurs but no one's seen one for millions of years. They're supposed to be extinct."

"If it is anything like a coelacanth, I bet it's not dangerous," said Marina. "I didn't have time to tell you earlier but I found the coelacanth. It was in the cave where I was trapped. It was timid and gentle – maybe this creature is just the same."

The megacoelacanthus, now the right way up again, came drifting towards the cave they were in.

"It doesn't matter how gentle it is, it's going to squash us if it tries to come in here!" cried Coralie.

"We've got to make it stop!" said Kai in alarm as their pets started to swim around in panic. The megacoelacanthus was getting closer.

Marina could see Coralie was right. But what could they do? Looking around desperately, Marina's eyes fell on the pot of mermaid fire just inside the cave entrance. She grabbed it and thrust it up towards the giant creature. Its huge eyes widened and it stopped in its tracks. Then it swam backwards, letting out a confused wail.

"Poor thing, it sounds so sad," said Luna.

"I think it's unhappy." Before anyone could stop her, she had ducked under Marina's arm and swum out of the cave.

"Luna, what are you doing?" cried Coralie in alarm. "Come back!"

But Luna ignored her. Marina's heart pounded as the younger mergirl swam up to the enormous creature's face. What if she was wrong about it being a gentle giant? What if the monster from the stories, which liked to eat merpeople, was really a megacoelacanthus?!

"Luna!" she shrieked as the creature's mouth yawned open.

But Luna just dived round its jaws and swam up to its enormous eyes. It blinked in surprise as if it had only just seen her.

"Hi, I'm Luna." Luna spoke softly. "I want to be your friend." She started to hum and began to stroke its cheek. Marina was sure it would hardly have been able to feel Luna's fingers through the thick scales but it shut its mouth and seemed to relax.

"Luna's working her magic," whispered
Coralie.

"Even dinosaur fish love her!" said Naya in
amazement.

Luna swam round its head, stroking it.
"Come and say hello," she called to the
others. "You're right, Marina. It is really
sweet and gentle."

They swam out of the cave. Suddenly there was the loud blast of a horn and the guards, led by Razeem, suddenly came charging through the water, tridents and harpoons raised.

The megacoelacanthus jumped and tried to swing round to swim away. Its armoured tail smashed into a tree, sending chunks of coral flying. Kai only just dodged out of the way in time.

"Attack the sea serpent, guards!" Razeem shouted, pointing at the terrified megacoelacanthus. "Attack it now!"

Chapter Ten
Home
Sweet Home

"No!" shrieked Luna. She flung her arms wide. "You mustn't hurt it! I won't let you! It doesn't mean any harm."

Marina raced to Luna's side. "Luna's right. Please don't attack," she begged. "It's not a sea serpent. We think it's a megacoelacanthus and it's very gentle."

"If you want to harpoon it, you'll have to harpoon me first!" shouted Luna.

"And us!" shouted Naya, Kai and Coralie, joining them in front of the megacoelacanthus.

"Kai?" exclaimed Indra. "What are you doing here?"

"Get away from the sea serpent!" Razeem commanded.

"It's not a sea serpent," repeated Marina.

"My daughter is right!"

Marina gasped as she saw her dad swimming towards them. "Tell the guards to lower their weapons at once, Razeem. That's no sea serpent – it is a megacoelacanthus. An ancient creature. It must have been living somewhere in the ocean, hidden from sight, and has somehow ended up here. It needs our help and protection, not to be attacked."

He reached them and shook his head in astonishment. "What's going on, Marina? Why are you out here?"

"I woke up and saw you were gone," she said. "I was worried so I came after you." She swam over and hugged him. "Oh, I'm so glad you're OK, Dad. I had a real adventure!

I started looking for you in the caves but then I got trapped in one. Luckily, Sami fetched the others and they got me out."

"Marina," her dad said, pulling her close. "You could have been injured. You really shouldn't have followed me, you know. I was planning on getting back before you woke up."

"I was worried about you because I didn't know where you were or what you were doing," Marina said.

"I was looking for that coelacanth you told me about but I didn't find it. Still, it seems you found something even more interesting!"

Tarak looked up at the megacoelacanthus

in awe. "I can't believe it," he said softly. "A living, breathing megacoelacanthus."

"It does explain the damage," said Indra, looking at the huge creature.

Luna swam back to the creature's head and stroked it. "He's very gentle," she said. "I'm sure he hasn't been damaging things on purpose. It's just he's so big he can't help but knock trees and stuff over."

The megacoelacanthus opened his mouth. The guards shrank back but all the creature did was let out a moaning cry again. Then he lowered his head and nudged his nose towards the damaged cave. "No, you can't go in there," Luna told him. "You won't fit." She bit her lip. "I think that's what he's been doing. He's been trying to get into a cave to hide."

"Or to find a way down to the quiet depths of the ocean," said Tarak.

"How did he end up here?" said Kai.

"I imagine that he was living in a remote, deep ocean but then something disturbed him," said Tarak. "Look." He swam up and plucked off some netting caught on one of the megacoelacanthus's fins. "Humans may have been starting to get closer to where he lived. He probably decided to leave his home to find somewhere quiet and peaceful."

"And ended up here," said Marina. "Poor thing." She swam to join Luna and stroked the giant fish's face. He closed his eyes happily.

"This is all very well and good," snapped Razeem, "but what are we going to do with it? If it stays here, it will destroy the reef."

"We could help him into the Abyss," said Tarak. "He'll be safe there."

"Maybe we could make one of the tunnels bigger?" suggested Naya. "Then he could swim down."

Tarak frowned. "That would take a long time."

"I know!" said Marina. "How about we use

Mermaids Rock?"

Everyone looked at her.

"The whirlpool can take creatures anywhere in the ocean by magic," Marina rushed on. "Why don't we ask it to transport him to the Abyss?"

"That's an excellent idea!" her father said, beaming at her.

"It's *squid-iculous*!" exclaimed Razeem. "How are we going to get this creature to the rock? We can hardly put it on a lead and swim it there!"

"No, we can't," agreed Luna. "But I think he might follow me." She patted the megacoelacanthus's face. "What do you think? Will you come with me?" She swam away a little and beckoned to him. "Come on!" She started humming again.

The megacoelacanthus began to follow the little mermaid.

Tarak put an arm round Marina and hugged her. "You know, I think this might just work!"

On the journey to Mermaids Rock, the megacoelacanthus knocked over quite a few more trees and flattened a lot of bushes. It looked around sadly at the trail of broken coral behind it. Marina felt very sorry for it. This world of delicate coral, sea sponges and anemones was no place for such a huge creature. He needed to be swimming in the wide, deep trenches of the Abyss.

When they arrived at Mermaids Rock, the sun was just coming up in the sky, making the water glitter and shine. The merpeople spotted the megacoelacanthus and hurried over to see what was going on, talking and exclaiming. The creature looked at them anxiously. Marina and the others swam up to its face to stroke and soothe it.

"Jumping jellyfish, what's that?"

"Is it a sea serpent?"

"Is it dangerous?"

Razeem blew his horn for quiet. "Please do not panic, everyone. There is no need to be alarmed. I found this creature on the deep reef…"

"I thought *we* found it," Coralie muttered to Marina.

"And so," continued Razeem, "I was able to work out what had been damaging the coral. It was clear to me from the moment I laid eyes on it that it meant us no harm…"

"Really?" Naya whispered to Marina.

"I have decided to help it by sending it to the Abyss where it can live quietly and peacefully," Razeem continued. He swam to the rock and touched it with his hand. "To the Abyss!" he commanded the whirlpool. The water at the base of the rock started to swirl faster and faster.

Luna kissed the creature's face. "It's time to go, Stanley. The whirlpool will take you somewhere you'll be safe."

"Stanley?" Marina said.

"That's what I'm calling him," said Luna. She kissed the megacoelacanthus again and he shut his eyes happily for a moment. When he opened them, Luna pointed at the swirling waters by Mermaids Rock. "Go on, Stanley! Go!"

The megacoelacanthus opened his mouth and let out a long, hopeful note.

"May the ocean keep you safe, my friend!" called Tarak.

Stanley lunged forwards through the water and dived head first into the whirlpool. His enormous body vanished, leaving just a trail of bubbles, which were quickly sucked up by the swirling water.

"He's gone," said Luna, catching her breath as the water started to slow down again.

"He'll be happy now though," said Marina, joining her and squeezing her hand.

"I wish I could have studied him some more," said her father wistfully.

"Don't worry, Dad. I've found something almost as good for you to study – the coelacanth. I know where it lives!" Marina said.

Her dad gaped. "What? Where?"

"I'll tell you but only if you promise that if you go out again at night you'll let me know first or at least leave me a note," she said.

"Of course I will." He kissed her forehead. "It was very brave of you to come after me and it worked out well because you were there to help the megacoelacanthus, but I really don't want you putting yourself in danger. From now on, I won't go out without telling you first, I promise."

Marina beamed at him. "In that case, you need to go and look in the damaged caves near where you found us. The one with a rockfall blocking its entrance has a crevice inside. It's where the coelacanth is living."

There was a splash and the next moment Marina's dad was swimming away towards the deep-water reef. Marina smiled. She had a feeling her dad was going to be just as happy as Stanley with an endangered coelacanth to study!

"My father has saved us all from the monster!" Glenda's triumphant voice rose above everyone else's. "My father's the best." She headed towards where the guards were now talking about how to repair the reef.

Catching sight of Marina and the others, she stopped. "What are you geeks and freaks doing out here?" she said haughtily.

"Well, actually, *we* just solved the mystery of the monster," said Coralie.

Marina grinned. "I guess you could say us geeks and freaks saved the day!"

"You lot?" scoffed Glenda. "You're just a bunch of gormless guppies!"

Before Marina could reply, Luna swam in front of her and glared up at Glenda. "Be quiet, Glenda! We don't care what you think of us so you can just go away. Oh, and by the way, when you do that, *you're* the one who looks like a gormless guppy!" she added as Glenda's mouth opened and shut like a fish.

The others burst out laughing. Looking furious, Glenda flounced away.

Coralie hugged her cousin. "Wow, Luna! That was *fin-tabulous*! I can't believe you just told Glenda Seaglass to get lost!"

Luna grinned. "After making friends with a megacoelacanthus and shouting at Chief Razeem, Glenda suddenly didn't seem that scary. I don't care any more if she thinks we're geeks and freaks."

Naya nodded. "Me neither. Being the way we are helped us save Stanley."

"We really do make a perfect mystery-solving team!" said Marina, happiness tingling from her head to her tail. "I think we should try to solve lots more mysteries in the future!"

Dash whistled excitedly, Tommy and Melly joined in by clapping their flippers, Octavia blew bubbles and Sami danced around in front of Marina's nose. She giggled. "Yes, you can all help too."

She held up her hand, palm outstretched to her friends. "Here's to our next adventure – let's hope it's not too far away!"

Her friends high-fived her. "To more adventures!" they shouted before falling backwards into the water.

"I need some breakfast," Kai said, flipping on to his tummy. "I'm so hungry I think I could eat a megacoelacanthus!"

"Ha! What would a megacoelacanthus do if Kai tried to eat him for breakfast?" Coralie said.

"What?" said Marina.

"He'd WHALE of course!" Coralie grinned.

They all groaned and splashed Coralie with their tails until she squealed and charged away. Giggling and chattering together, they raced after her through the shimmering, sunlit water.

Turn the page to learn more about Marina's beautiful home and the creatures that live there!

THE AMAZING OCEAN

70% of the surface of the Earth is covered in water and oceans contain 97% of the Earth's water!

Scientists estimate that humans still have around 95% of the world's oceans yet to explore – there's so much out there to discover! This explains why it's impossible to know how many species live in the ocean. It is estimated that 91% of ocean species are yet to be classified.

Not only does the ocean contain an incredible variety of wildlife, we can also learn a lot about our history through the artefacts and remnants that can be found in the ocean. There are more artefacts in the oceans than in all of the museums in the world combined!

The oceans cover a huge amount of our planet, and as well as being wide they're also incredibly deep! The average depth of the ocean is 12,100 feet and the deepest part of the ocean is 36,200 feet deep and can be found beneath the western Pacific Ocean.

CORAL KINGDOMS

Coral reefs only make up 0.1% of the oceans, but they support 25% of the planet's marine species!

Often called the rainforests of the sea, coral reefs not only support marine life, but humans rely on them for their livelihoods, nutrition, protection from storms and the economic opportunities they provide.

Coral reefs are made up of corals, which are living creatures and relatives of jellyfish and anemones! They have existed for 400 million years, despite being very fragile.

Reef-growing corals are found in shallow, tropical waters of around 20-29 °C. They're very sensitive to temperature change, which is why climate change is such a threat.

Alongside climate change, overfishing, tourism and pollution, among other things, damage coral reefs. So far 19% of the world's reefs have been lost.

SAVE THE SEA CREATURES CLUB

As you can see, the ocean and coral reefs
are a vital part of our planet and affect all
creatures great and small! What can we do to
help? Here are a few ideas...

Climate change is currently the biggest threat
to the coral reefs. We can help by saving
energy and reducing our carbon footprints.
We can do this by making small changes,
such as walking or riding bikes, taking public
transport rather than driving and turning off
lights when we leave a room.

Single use plastic is making its way into the oceans and can harm the beautiful creatures that live there. Try and avoid plastic by using reusable water bottles and bags, and recycling whenever possible.

When you've been out and about, make sure you clean up and take your rubbish with you! It's also important to not only take your own rubbish, but to clear up any other rubbish that you might see. Another way to help would be to organize or take part in beach clean ups and litter picks.

Oceans are beautiful and fascinating – if you're lucky enough to get the chance, take time to explore them and see their wonders for yourself! But make sure not to touch the coral reefs, or to take any corals or rocks away with you, as this can damage them.

MEET SAMI
THE SEAHORSE

Seahorses are tiny fish, ranging from
two to thirty-five centimetres in length.

They can live up to three years in the wild.

Female seahorses lay eggs in a pouch
on the male seahorse – then it can take up to
forty-five days until they hatch.

Seahorses can camouflage themselves,
which helps them to hide from predators.
It also helps them to be predators as well!
They can hide until their prey swims by –
then they suck the food through their
mouths and swallow them whole!

LEARN MORE ABOUT ELUSIVE COELACANTHS!

Coelacanths – known as living fossils –
were thought to have gone extinct with the
dinosaurs sixty-five million years ago but in
1938 this was proved not to be the case when
one was discovered in the Indian Ocean.

They can live for up to sixty years in the wild
and measure about 6.5 feet. They are really
heavy too, weighing up to 90 kilograms!

Coelacanths hide in underwater caves
during the day and come out to feed at night.
They can live in depths of up to 2,300 feet.

These are just some of the reasons Tarak was
so excited to find the coelacanth!

About the Author

Linda Chapman is the best-selling
author of over 200 books. The biggest
compliment Linda can receive is for a
child to tell her they became a reader
after reading one of her books.
Linda lives in a cottage with a tower in
Leicestershire with her husband, three
children, three dogs and two ponies.
When she's not writing, Linda likes to
ride, read and visit schools and libraries
to talk to people about writing.

www.lindachapmanauthor.co.uk

About the Illustrator

Mirelle Ortega is a Mexican artist based in Los Angeles. She has a MFA in Visual Development from the Academy of Art University in San Francisco. Mirelle loves magic, vibrant colours and ghost stories. But more than anything, she loves telling unique stories with funny characters and a touch of magical realism.

www.mirelleortega.com

JOIN MARINA AND HER
FRIENDS FOR THEIR NEXT
ADVENTURE IN...

MERMAIDS ROCK

The Floating Forest

COMING SOON!